Robin Hill School

Wash Your Hands!

written by Margaret McNamara
illustrated by Mike Gordon

Ready-to-Read

Simon Spotlight

New York   London   Toronto   Sydney

In memory of Ann Reit
– M. M.

Simon Spotlight
An imprint of Simon & Schuster Children's Publishing Division
1230 Avenue of the Americas, New York, NY 10020
Text copyright © 2010 by Margaret McNamara
Illustrations copyright © 2010 by Mike Gordon
All rights reserved, including the right of reproduction in
whole or in part in any form.
SIMON SPOTLIGHT, READY-TO-READ, and colophon are registered
trademarks of Simon & Schuster, Inc.
For information about special discounts for bulk purchases, please contact Simon &
Schuster Special Sales at 1-866-506-1949 or business@simonandschuster.com.
The Simon & Schuster Speakers Bureau can bring authors to your live event. For more
information or to book an event contact the Simon & Schuster Speakers Bureau at
1-866-248-3049 or visit our website at www.simonspeakers.com.
Manufactured in the United States of America 0320 LAK
10 9
Library of Congress Cataloging-in-Publication Data
McNamara, Margaret.
Wash your hands! / by Margaret McNamara ; illustrated by Mike Gordon. – 1st Simon
Spotlight pbk. [ed.]
p. cm. – (Robin Hill School) (Ready-to-read)
Summary: When everyone in Mrs. Connor's first grade class has a cold, she shows her
students how to wash their hands to get rid of germs.
ISBN 978-1-4169-9172-4
[1. Hand washing–Fiction. 2. Schools–Fiction.] I. Gordon, Mike, 1948 Mar. 16- ill. II. Title.
PZ7.M47879343Was 2010   [E]–dc22   2009044211

Everyone in Mrs. Connor's class had a cold.

Nick sneezed.

Jamie coughed.

Emma blew.

"We have a lot of germs
in our classroom,"
said Mrs. Connor.

"I do not see any germs," said Michael.

"Germs are too small to see," said Mrs. Connor.

"But germs are powerful. They can make you sick."

"I am sick of this cold,"
said Nick.

"If I could see those germs,
I would beat them up!"

"I know a good way
to get rid of germs,"
said Mrs. Connor.

"Who would like
to show me
how to wash hands?"
she asked.

"I will!" said Reza.

He turned on the cold water and stuck his hands underneath.

"Done!" he said.

"You forgot the soap,"
said Nia.

She pumped out a little soap
and rinsed her hands.

"Done!" she said.

"You both did a good job,"

said Mrs. Connor.

"But not a good enough job
to get rid of germs."

"The best way
to get rid of germs,"
she said, "is to sing."
"Sing?" asked the class.

Mrs. Connor said,
"Roll up your sleeves,
please."

She turned on warm water
and gave everyone
some soap.

Then Mrs. Connor sang:
"Wash your hands
with soap each time . . .

. . . and remember
this short rhyme.
Let the water
run real warm.

Stop those germs
from doing harm.

Keep on washing,
make it fun.

Now you know
just how it's done."

"That is the ABC song!"

said Becky.

"Now it is the
Wash Hands song,"
said Jamie.

The first graders sang
the Wash Hands song
every time they washed
their hands.

Soon everybody got better.
"I told you I could
beat those germs,"
said Nick.